Nothing in my life has had more impact or been more meaningful than experiencing the love of my sweet maternal grandmother - Flora Bell Carlton. Yes, I think all would agree that grandparents by their very nature are wonderful in every way, and I can't help but believe my grandmother was the best one of all!

Grandma, as I called her, was a simple woman, not formally educated, never gained financial wealth, was never famous in any way, and loved only one man for a lifetime - my grandfather, Marvin Carlton. She was everything to me.

Like it was yesterday, I can remember the anticipation that would build when I knew I was going to be with my grandmother for the weekend. Life for the weekend would be wonderful in every way. She always made me feel like I was the most important and most loved person in the world.

Grandma was the cornerstone of our family. In my entire life, I never heard anyone speak a negative word of her. She lived a remarkable life and, without question, made this world a better place.

I wrote this story to share the very essence of this special magic called Camp Nana Papa. As the story reveals, Camp Nana Papa is not an actual place at all, it is the magic that lives in the "heart" of every grandparent and grandchild.

In her honor, I dedicate this book to a most wonderful and pure woman, my grandmother - Flora Bell Carlton.

A special thank you to: Jeff Ebbeler - the illustrator

My words fail when I try to say thank you enough and honor the exceptional work of Jeff Ebbeler, a most talented artist. He has wonderfully brought the characters and story to life in the eyes of the reader. Jeff, you far exceeded my expectations. I am looking forward to our many projects of the future!

I invite everyone to visit Jeff's website to enjoy his many works and gain further appreciation for his gift of art - www.jeffillustration.com. The best of the best.

A very special thank you to my friend Mike Massengale who helped create our special friend and adorable character "Flash the Firefly" and for being a part of the fantastic storyboard creation where it all started. You know my respect for your work and even more importantly the person that you are as a father, husband, and artist.

Thank you to everyone who supported and encouraged me and gave their input on how to best tell this story.

# THE ADVENTURES OF

by Donnie Cranfill

illustrated by Jeffrey Ebbeler

The Adventures of Camp Nana Papa™

Requests to the Publisher for permission should be addressed to the Permission Department,
Grand Ventures LLC
172 East Main Street
Spartanburg, SC 29306
or online at grandservice@campnanapapa.com

Published by Grand Ventures LLC
172 East Main Street
Spartanburg, SC 29306

www.campnanapapa.com

ISBN – 978-0-692-57885-8 - hard cover

Book design by Jeffrey Ebbeler.

The illustrations are rendered in acrylic paint on paper.

Second Edition

Printed and bound in the
United States of America
by Versa Press
East Peoria, IL
© 2016

www.campnanapapa.com

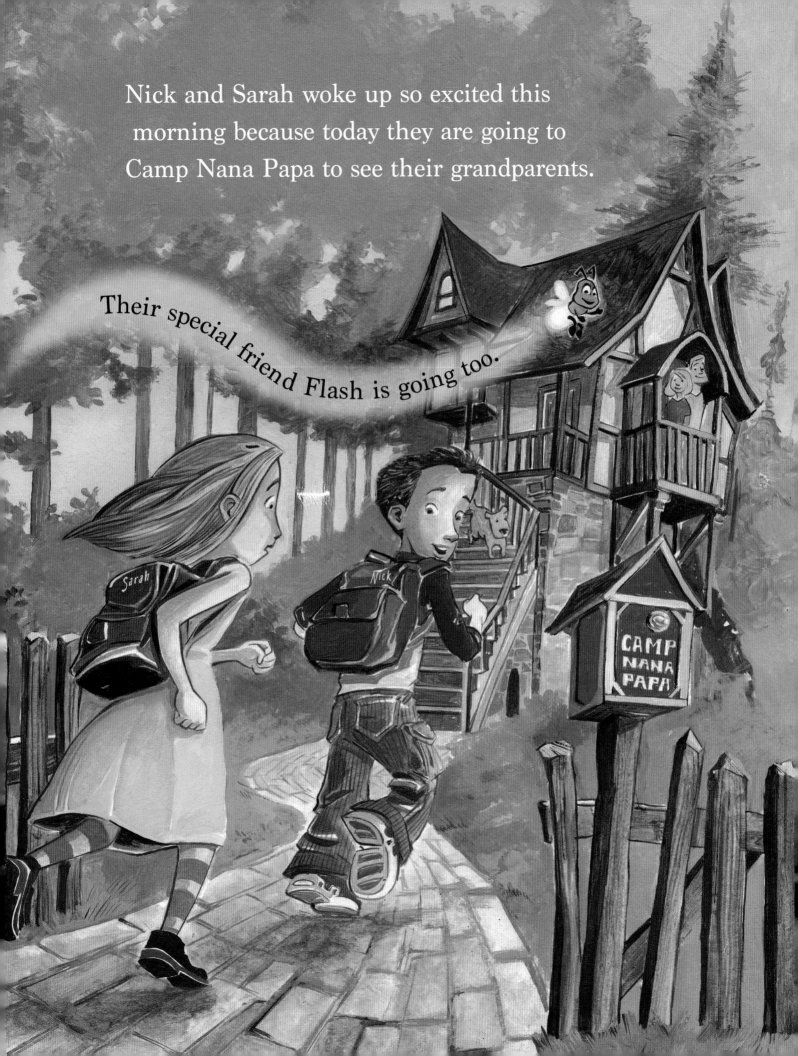

Nick and Sarah woke up so excited this
morning because today they are going to
Camp Nana Papa to see their grandparents.

Their special friend Flash is going too.

CAMP
NANA
PAPA

What is Camp Nana Papa?

It's the magic that lives in the "heart" of every grandchild and grandparent. Anytime children are with, or even thinking about their grandparents, that is Camp Nana Papa. Nick and Sarah have always called time with their grandparents Camp Nana Papa.

Nick and Sarah have many friends, and they love
Camp Nana Papa too. Sometimes kids use other
names for their grandparents like: Grandma and
Grandpa, Gi-Gi and Paw-Paw, and even Me-Maw
and Pops. What do you call your grandparents?

The first time Nick and Sarah met Flash, they were at Camp Nana Papa. Now Flash is their best friend and goes everywhere with them.

Nick and Sarah are always excited when they get to spend the night ... and sometimes even the whole weekend at Camp Nana Papa. They have their own special tent that Nana and Papa gave them. Tonight they are having fun camping and roasting marshmallows by the warm fire.

Nick and Sarah love running and catching fireflies. Look! There are fireflies everywhere.

Flash's little light is always so bright. He guides Nick and Sarah in the night to find all of his firefly friends. Nick and Sarah try to see who can catch the most. Of course, after catching and playing with them, Nick and Sarah open their jars and let the fireflies go, so they can catch them again!

After a night of camping, Nick and Sarah are ready to play games.

Flash likes to play along too.

Sarah likes kick-ball the most!

Nana and Papa have a beautiful dog named River. Nick and Sarah always look forward to playing with him.

He runs so fast!

With Nana and Papa there are so many fun things to do:

Swimming ...

After playing games outside in the hot sun, swimming and splashing in Nana and Papa's pool make Nick and Sarah laugh.

Fishing ...

Papa has a big boat and loves to fish.
Nick is catching his very first fish.
Does Flash have one too?

Visiting the zoo ...

TICKETS

ZOO

There are animals everywhere! Nick's favorite animal is the polar bear, and Sarah's is the giraffe.

# Eating ice cream ...

It always seems to taste better
at Camp Nana Papa.
Nana gives them so much!

That is one big sandcastle Nick and Sarah
are building. Flash is king of the castle!

After a day of Camp Nana Papa fun, Nick and Sarah are always ready for some goodies. Nana's cookies are the best. She helps Nick and Sarah make their own.

At the end of the day, it is time to go to bed.
Nothing is better than when Nana reads a
bedtime story.  Sarah giggles and smiles at Nana
because Nick almost always falls asleep first.

The time comes when Nick and Sarah have to go back home. Even before leaving Camp Nana Papa, they get excited thinking about coming back. They are making their list of fun things to do next time. There's no place they love more.

When you grow up, maybe you will have children. And, guess what? They will love their grandparents too! All children love being with their grandparents, that's why all kids love Camp Nana Papa!

Next time you are at Camp Nana Papa, maybe you

can go fishing,

catch some fireflies,

eat some warm cookies,

or have your grandparent read a favorite bedtime story.

Nick and Sarah have to say goodbye for now, but their hearts are happy because they know soon they will return to their favorite place in the world -

Camp Nana Papa.

# My Camp Nana Papa Badge

Name _ _ _ _ _ _ _ _ _ _ _ _ _

# I call my grandparents...

- - - - - - - - - - - - - - - - - - - -

My Mother's Mother

- - - - - - - - - - - - - - - - - - - -

My Mother's Father

- - - - - - - - - - - - - - - - - - - -

My Father's Mother

- - - - - - - - - - - - - - - - - - - -

My Father's Father

# How big were you the first time you read about Flash and Camp Nana Papa?

Can you draw your hand?

# what is your favorite thing to do at your Camp Nana Papa?

Flash really likes fishing.

Flash likes to swim too.

And eat cookies!

# If you had a friend like Flash what would it look like?

Can you draw Flash a friend?

# What are you going to do at your Camp Nana Papa next time?

1. _____

2. _____

3. _____

4. _____

5. _____

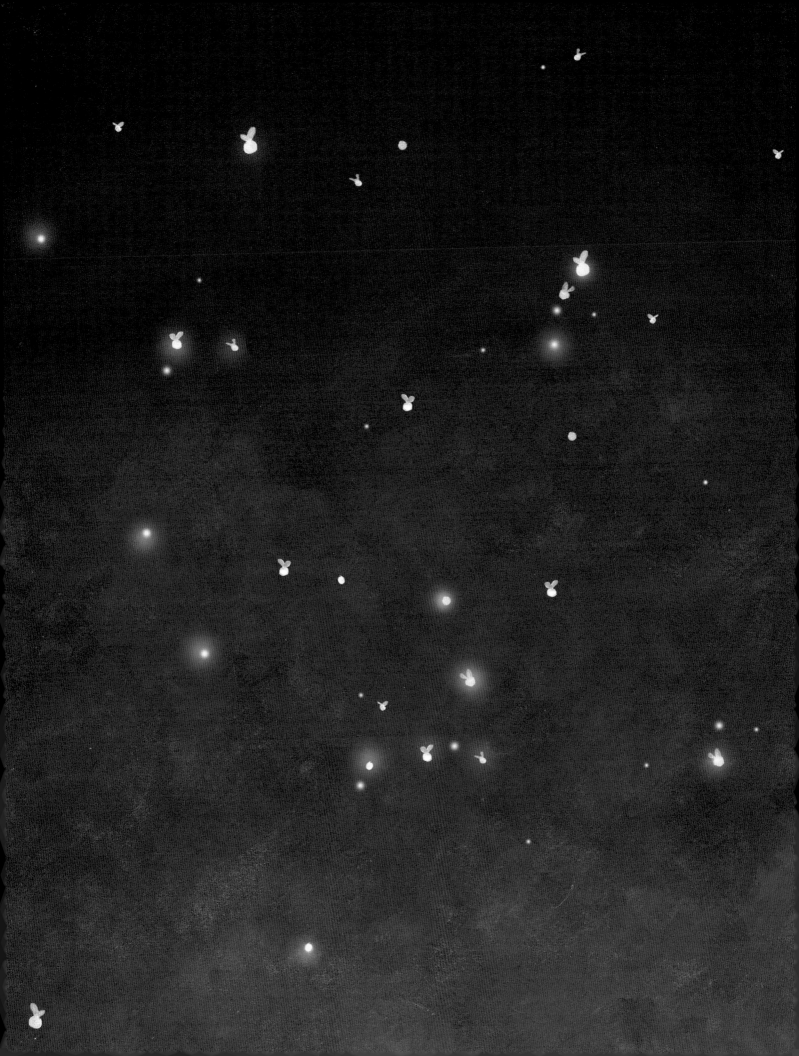